Y. FRI
Prejudice
CF

ISBN: 1-903078-11-3

© Siphano Picture Books, 1999 for the text and illustrations
First published in Great Britain in 1999 by Siphano Picture Books Ltd.

www.siphano.com

Colour separation: Vivliosynergatiki, Athens, Greece
Printed in Italy by Grafiche AZ, Verona

Claudia Fries

A PIG IS MOVING IN!

SIPHANO PICTURE BOOKS
London

One morning, as Henrietta Hen was hanging out
her washing, Doctor Fox greeted her with exciting news.
"Our new neighbour is moving into our block of flats today!"
he said.

"Oh dear," said Henrietta. "I hope it is someone quiet
and tidy."

Nick Hare popped his head out of the window.
"A clean cat or an orderly mole would be nice…"

Soon they heard the new tenant arriving.

Nick Hare, Doctor Fox and Henrietta Hen all hid at the top of the stairs to get a glimpse of their new neighbour. When they saw him, they couldn't believe their eyes! He was not a clean cat, he was not an orderly mole, nor was he a fox, a hen or a hare.

"Oh my!" gasped Henrietta. "It's … a Pig! A Pig is moving in! That won't do at all. Everyone knows that pigs are messy and dirty and sloppy." Doctor Fox and Nick Hare nodded in agreement.

Later that day, Doctor Fox met the Pig carrying firewood.
Doctor Fox walked on fast and didn't say "hello",
but he *did* slow down enough to see what the Pig was up to.
And he wasn't a bit surprised when the Pig dropped some
pieces of wood on the pavement outside.

Doctor Fox went and complained to Henrietta Hen.

"What a mess!" he said. "That Pig has left wood all over our pavement."

"Oh dear," said Henrietta. She went out and looked, but she couldn't see any wood.

"Doctor Fox must have swept it up," she thought.

But it was the Pig who had swept up the mess. Then he went up to his flat to build a nice warm fire.

Next it was Henrietta Hen's turn to meet the Pig. He was
carrying two heavy bags of groceries. She didn't say "hello"
to him either, but she *did* sneak under the stairs to see
what the Pig would do this time. And she wasn't a bit surprised
when he dropped a bag of flour at the bottom of the stairs.
It burst open with a *puff* and a *splat!*

Henrietta Hen went and complained to Nick Hare.

"What a mess!" she said. "That Pig has left our entrance hall covered in flour."

"How dreadful!" exclaimed Nick. He went out and looked, but couldn't see any flour.

"Henrietta must have cleaned it up," he thought.

But it was the Pig who had swept and mopped up the floor. Then he went into his kitchen to bake cinnamon biscuits.

Not long after, Nick Hare met the Pig. He walked slowly
behind the Pig so that he wouldn't have to say "hello",
but he *did* wait to see what would happen. He couldn't believe
what he saw: the Pig was carrying mud into his flat! The mud
was dripping on the floor and Pig was walking through it,
leaving a trail of trotter-prints behind him.

Nick Hare went and complained
to Doctor Fox and Henrietta Hen.

"What a mess!" he said. "That Pig has left mud all over
our stairs!"

"Disgusting!" agreed Doctor Fox and Henrietta Hen,
shaking their heads. But when they went out and looked, they
couldn't see any mud.

"Nick must have cleaned it up," they said.

But it was Pig who had washed the stairs three times over.
And it wasn't mud, it was clay. Pig was taking it up
to his workshop to make pottery.

"That does it," decided Henrietta, Nick and Doctor Fox. "If a Pig wants to live in our block of flats, he must behave properly. Otherwise, he will have to go!"

And off they went upstairs, to tell him.

They rang the bell. *Ding-dong! Ding-dong! Ding-dong!*

"Oh … hello!" said the Pig. He was surprised to have visitors so soon.

Doctor Fox, Henrietta Hen and Nick Hare were just about to start complaining, when the door opened wider. A sweet smell of cinnamon floated out, and they heard a fire crackling in Pig's sitting-room.

"We noticed a mess in the hallway…" began Doctor Fox.

"Oh, I *do* apologise," said the Pig, "and I do hope I've cleaned everything up thoroughly …"

Doctor Fox, Henrietta Hen and Nick Hare looked at each other in surprise.

"So it wasn't you who swept up the wood!" said Henrietta to Doctor Fox.

"And it wasn't you who mopped up the flour!" said Nick to Henrietta.

"And it wasn't you who washed away the muddy trotter-prints!" said Doctor Fox and Henrietta to Nick Hare.

They all shook their heads, as they realised that the Pig had cleaned everything up himself…

"My name is Theodore," said the Pig. "Will you join me for tea?"

So they did. Doctor Fox, Henrietta Hen and Nick Hare went into Theodore's bright, clean kitchen and helped him get tea ready. They couldn't help admiring the cups and pots that he had made in his workshop.

"I have a new board game we could play," said Theodore. When he got it out, Henrietta was flattered to see that he had made a special playing-piece for each of his new neighbours.

"You have a lovely flat, Theodore," said Nick Hare, tucking into another biscuit.

"It's a beautiful flat," echoed Doctor Fox and Henrietta Hen. They were imagining all the cosy afternoon teas they were going to spend together.

What a wonderful new neighbour they had!